DEDICATION

Thank you to my many readers who have followed Cam Derringer through the years.

I have been asked to write a prequel to the series so you would know more about how Cam grew up. I hope you enjoy this book.

There are many more to come.

BOOKS BY MAC FORTNER

A DARK NIGHT IN KEY WEST
SERIES PREQUEL

BY

Mac Fortner

COVER DESIGN BY MAC FORTNER

WEBSITE: www.macofortner.com

ISBN: 9781726837514

DISCLAIMER

The characters and events portrayed in this book are a work of fiction or are used fictitiously. Any similarity to real persons, living or dead, is coincidental and not intended by the author.

A DARK NIGHT IN KEY WEST

PROLOGUE

I was walking home after a game of baseball we had played in the street in front of Billy Day's house. It was dark, and I should have been home thirty minutes ago.

A light from a window caught my attention as I passed the house of another friend. In the small, conch style clapboard house, maintenance seemed neglected. The paint was chipping off, and weeds were taking over what little yard there was.

I saw a man standing outside the lit-up window looking in. He wasn't even trying to hide the fact that he didn't belong there and that he was *peeping* in her window.

I thought it strange that the light would be on and the shades lifted.

I knew the girl who lived there. She was in my fifth-grade class at Lower Key Grade School. She was twelve years old and had long brown hair. Her name was Susie Towns. I always thought she was a pretty girl if you liked girls. I was starting to take a little interest in them myself. I had heard that her mother ran away with a fisherman and left Susie here with her father.

The man took a few more steps closer to the window. He reached into his pocket and pulled out a pack of cigarettes, shook one up and pulled it from the pack. He lit it, cupping his hand around the flame to hide the glow.

He took another step toward the window.

"Hey!" I yelled.

He snapped around and looked my way. Then he turned back toward the window.

"Hey!" I yelled again.

He glanced my way once more. That's when the light caught his face, and I saw my teacher, Mr. Powers.

"Get out of here, kid," he said in a low gruff voice.

Unaware that I could see his face; he seemed to be trying to disguise his voice. He turned back toward the window. That's when I saw him unzip his pants and reach inside.

I picked up a rock and, running toward him, I hurled it at the window to warn Susie. The rock hit the window, and the glass shattered. Mr. Powers turned and ran away from me, disappearing down the alley.

I went to the window. That was my *first mistake*. Susie was in front of the window, naked. Her father had her arms locked behind her with his large hands, holding her still. Susie had a look of shock and embarrassment on her face. Her father's eyes were wide, like someone caught in, well, caught in the act of committing a crime, I guess.

"Sorry," was all I could utter. Not that they could have heard me mumbling.

I didn't know what else to say because I couldn't comprehend what it was I was seeing.

I ran hard and fast. I didn't stop running until I reached the park two blocks away. I sat down at a picnic table to catch my breath. I was going to be in big trouble. I had broken a window and I had seen my teacher watching – watching what? Susie's father holding her still so Mr. Powers could look at her? I think so.

I walked the rest of the way home, hiding as best I could. Over the years, I never said anything to anyone about that night, and no one ever said anything to me either. Susie didn't look me in the eyes again for a long time. Neither did Mr. Powers.

At the end of the school year when we received our report cards, mine had all 'A's. I knew I didn't deserve them, but I let it go. That was the first time I ever took a payoff and the last. It made me feel as if I were a part of the perverted crime that took place in front of me.

That night haunted me for years. How could a father do that? Over the years, I heard that there had been a child porn ring in Key

West. My guess is that's what I happened upon that night.

There were reports of young – the youngest rumored to be six – children sold to the highest bidder for one night at a time. Some children were never seen again. Their families had to try to hide the crimes because they were directly responsible for the missing children. The word was that whoever rented them for the night would sometimes take them to Miami and sell them. It was a bad time in the streets of Key West. All of us had a friend, brother, or sister that had disappeared, and the rumors were that they had been a victim. I was lucky I came from a good family.

I remember in our junior year of high school, Susie showing up several times with bruises on her arms and legs. One day I stopped her and asked if everything was all right. She just stared at me. Her eyes looked sad. I think she wanted to say something but couldn't. I reached out to take her hand and she gave it to me willingly. We walked to our next class together, not saying anything.

After school that day, I walked her home, still not speaking. Her father was sitting on the front porch when we arrived. He gave me a hard look. He was no good, and I knew it. Sometimes you can tell just by looking at someone, and this was one of those times. I wanted to kill him, and a year later, the opportunity presented itself.

Chapter 1

Susie had to sneak out of the house on the nights we would meet. We were seniors now, and she was turning into a beautiful girl. Her brown hair lay in loose curls on her delicate shoulders. Her jaw was strong, her green eyes bright and her touch was soft and gentle. I felt as if I were pulled into her soul when she touched her lips to mine. I couldn't help myself. I think I loved her.

I had reached six-foot-two inches and weighed one hundred-eighty-five pounds. (I would eventually grow two inches taller and gain – well, we won't go there, but I'd gain weight.)

I didn't pressure her, but I dropped subtle hints that she was safe to tell me what had happened when I'd seen her through the window. She always changed the subject and turned away, pretending she didn't know what I was suggesting. Except for one night. Her face reddened, and her lips tightened. Her voice squeaked when she told me her father had made her stand nude in front of men while they took pictures. Sometimes they did other things. She didn't go into details about that, but I knew.

At eighteen, she wasn't as popular with the older men as she once was. Her father had made his money with her while he could. He drank his sin money, and he was intoxicated most of the time.

One day after I walked her home from school, her father asked me what my intentions were with his daughter. I told him they were to keep her safe. He laughed.

"She's a whore, you know," he said.

I told him I didn't think he should talk about her that way. I said, "She's only a victim of an abusive piece of shit, pimping father."

He hit me hard in the jaw. He was a big man, and I was still a skinny young boy of eighteen, but I had grit. I came back at him with a flurry of fists and kicks that caught him just right. He went down, and I jumped on top of him. That was my *second mistake.*

I should have kept my distance and punched when I could because once he had a grip on me I didn't have a chance. He beat me until my eyes swelled shut. Then while I was lying in the yard, I heard him beating Susie.

She finally quit crying.

I regained my footing and went toward them. Susie lay on the porch, her face red and unrecognizable. I was sure she was dead: she *couldn't* be alive. Her father, still on top of her, kept hitting her. I kicked him again to try to get him to leave her alone. I received another hard fist to the nose for my trouble.

When I fell off the porch, I landed on something hard -- a baseball bat. Though I could barely see, I felt it beneath me. I grabbed it and limped toward them again. Her father saw me coming and chuckled.

"Thanks, son," he said still laughing, "I could use that thing."

He obviously didn't expect me to be so fast. I swung the bat and felt it connect with his head. I only had to hit him once to get him to leave her alone. While he lay on his back, eyes open, staring at nothing, I went to Susie. I was right about her; she was dead. My heart ached. I wanted to tear it out.

The police arrived with an ambulance right behind them. While they put me on a gurney and loaded me in the back, I heard them say the other two were dead before I passed out.

I was not held responsible for any of the violence that took place that day. It seems a neighbor saw the whole thing and finally called 911. Why he didn't come help us, I don't know, but I made a silent oath to never let anyone hurt like that again if I could prevent it.

My name is Cam Derringer, and this wasn't my last war.

Chapter 2

I was born and raised in the beautiful, and colorful, town of Key West Florida. I love living here and I hope I always will.

I left Key West briefly to attend Yale University where I studied law and eventually received my degree. I was a sophomore at Yale when I met Malinda, my soulmate.

Malinda was sitting at the bar with some friends, sipping on a glass of beer. I knew who she was because I asked a friend of hers and was told she was dating no one.

I was enamored. *This is a girl I could fall in love with*, I told myself. And I did, but not before spilling my beer on her and then also knocking *her* glass of beer off the bar and into her lap. I really know how to make a good first impression.

I would never forget about Susie, never, but I survived that day and life goes on. I would learn that lesson again and again, for the rest of my life.

"I'm so sorry," I said to the beautiful girl with the beer on her blouse and in her lap.

She picked up her friend's beer, stood and slowly poured it over my head. When she finished she sat the glass back down on the bar.

I just stared at her for a moment, then smiled and said, "Do you come here often?"

We were married three years later and moved back to Key West after I finished my degree and passed the Bar Exam.

I could never live anywhere else, and luckily, Malinda loved it here.

I opened my law office with an old friend and mentor, Jim Dade. Life was good, and we were making money hand over fist. Yet, most importantly, we were happy.

Jim and his wife Terri had a daughter, Diane who was five years old when we started our practice. Malinda and I were always happy to babysit when they needed a night out on the town.

We couldn't have children of our own, so we spoiled Diane.

We enjoyed life, for a while.

Randy and Larry Higgins did some of their drinking at home, but most of it was at The Crab Leg Saloon.

On July fourth, they were celebrating with their friends at the bar. Larry and George Tally started telling lies about how fast their cars were.

"I've never been beaten in a quarter mile," George bragged.

He had never raced anyone for a quarter mile, so he really wasn't lying.

Larry slammed a twenty-dollar bill down on the bar and said, "You're on chump."

They lined up their cars on Highway One, just north of Key West. They couldn't stop in the middle of the road because of the traffic, so they rolled slowly until they were even with each other.

Randy was in the car behind them with three of their friends. It was agreed that the second car would honk when the race was to start.

The horn sounded, and the pedals went to the floor.

Neither car was particularly fast. For a few seconds, you couldn't really tell they were even racing. As time went on though, the cars reached the break-neck speed of eighty-five miles per hour. That was fast for this section of Highway One.

Jim and Terri came out of a gas station on Stock Island on their way to our friends for fireworks. Diane rode with Malinda and me a mile behind them.

When we arrived at the scene, it was hard to tell what we were looking at. Two cars lay turned upside down and another faced us on its side across the highway. People ran from one car to another.

"That doesn't look good, Cam," Malinda said.

I was about to say, "No it doesn't," when I recognized one of the cars: Jim and Terri's.

Malinda took Diane home with her and held her all night. I went to the hospital with

Jim, who had a broken arm. Terri never knew what hit her.

Diane was fourteen when her mother died in that crash. Malinda did her best to fill the void in Diane's life created from Terri's death. We were all devastated, but as I said, life goes on.

While Jim grieved, I took over the workload at the office for the next three months.

Jim returned one day and said he was ready to get on with his life. He had a daughter to think of. I should have insisted he take more time.

The same day Jim returned, we had a client appointed to us by the court. I took the case in order to give Jim a chance to settle back in.

It seems the man was arrested on drug charges and his bail had been met. Somewhat of a normal case, I thought, until I investigated it more closely.

"Good afternoon Mr. Dallas," I said standing to shake his hand.

"Mr. Derringer," he said nodding his head.

He was a slightly overweight man around six-foot. His hair was receding in the front, but he made up for it in the back where he had a frizzy ponytail. He *looked* like a drug dealer.

I checked over his file for a minute, then closed it.

"You sold cocaine to a police officer," I stated.

"So?" he said. "The guy didn't look like a police officer."

"Yes," I said. "That's called 'being under-cover.'"

"Is that legal?"

"Apparently, it is, Allen."

"Al," he said.

"Al."

"I should have just killed him when he pulled out his badge," Dallas said nonchalantly.

"Killed him?" I said.

"Yeah, the fuckin' jerk."

"If you would have *killed* him, we wouldn't be having this conversation. He wasn't alone. You would have been killed yourself."

"Big deal," he said. "People get killed all the time."

"Why are you telling me all this?"

"You can't tell anyone. You're my lawyer," he said and laughed. "It's a bitch knowing you might be defending a murderer and not be able to say anything about it, ain't it?"

"I'm defending a drug dealer," I said. "Whatever else you do isn't my business."

But it is. I can't let a murderer out on the street. I have to find a way to prove this guy might have killed someone. He's right though. I can't tell anyone what he tells me.

"You have a plea hearing set for two weeks," I said. "If you plead guilty, you'll probably get a year in prison and a year probation since this is your first offense."

"Fuck you," he said. "I ain't goin' to prison."

"Well, I hate to be the bearer of bad news, but they have you dead to rights."

He grunted.

"If you don't plead guilty, they won't be happy. You'll cost the court money. You'll probably get three to five years."

Dallas pointed one long crooked finger at me and said, “You’re my fuckin’ lawyer and you better get me out of this, or I might add you to my collection.”

“Your collection?” I asked.

He chortled and stood his ground.

“See ya, wouldn’t want to be ya,” he said as he walked out the door.

Chapter 3

When Dallas left, I filled Jim in on our new client.

"Sounds to me like he *wants* you to tell someone," he said.

"Yeah, then he can walk on a technicality."

"So, what do you wanna do?"

"I wanna see him fry," I said.

"Why don't you call Ron Stiller? I'll bet he'll find something on him," Jim said.

"Good thought. He's discreet and thorough; I'll call him."

Jim looked back down at the paperwork that had been piling on his desk.

"You need some help?" I asked.

"Tracy's coming in in a few minutes. I asked her to help," he said. "She's a good assistant. I don't know if we could get along without her."

"If you need anything," I said, "I'll be right next door."

"I'll be fine," he said. "There is one thing though. I want you and Malinda to come over tomorrow for Diane's birthday."

"I wouldn't miss it for the world. We already have the presents."

Diane looked beautiful for a fifteen-year-old girl, even with all the pain she had suffered through in the last three months.

"Uncle Cam!" she yelled as I entered, and she threw her arms around me.

I held her tight. I loved this girl, and I haven't been able to spend as much time with her as I would like.

We had supper, and then Malinda brought out the cake.

Diane closed her eyes and was still for a moment. Then she blew out the candles.

"Hope my wish comes true," she said.

"Let me guess," I said. "World peace."

"That goes unsaid, but not this time," she said. "I can't tell you, or it won't come true."

Diane opened her presents. She was ecstatic about the clothes and make-up Malinda bought for her.

"They're beautiful," she said.

Jim had bought her a very nice necklace with matching earrings.

"Thank you, Daddy," she said and hugged him.

Then she looked at me.

"What?" I said.

"That's okay, Cam. You didn't need to get me anything," she said. "I have everything I'll ever need."

"Well," I said. "Then I guess it's okay if I take that cruiser back you wanted."

Diane jumped up and ran to the window to look in the front yard.

"Hunt-uh," I said shaking my head.

She ran to the back window to look.

"Not back there either," I said. "If you leave it outside, someone will steal it."

She ran to the garage door and opened it.

I could hear her scream. "It's just the color I wanted!"

She ran back in and hugged me. I looked away hiding the tears forming in my eyes.

"You be careful riding that and wear your helmet."

"I'll buy one tomorrow," she said.

"There's still a present over there you haven't opened," I said.

She grabbed the box and ripped the paper off.

"A helmet," she said.

She put it on and wore it the rest of the night.

We took Diane out for ice cream, even though she already had cake.

"Where do you put all that food?" I asked her.

She flexed her muscles and said, "This doesn't just happen."

For a thin little girl, she did have some guns on her.

Ron Stiller called me the next day.

"Where'd you find this guy?" he asked.

"He was a present from the court."

"If I were you I wouldn't be buying any of the court officials any gifts for Christmas this year."

"That bad, huh," I said.

"Worse. This guy was questioned and released on the disappearance of three college girls. He was the only suspect, and the girls were never found."

"Wow. Why was he released?"

"No proof. They only got him in the first place because he was caught trying to coax another girl into his car. Two of her boyfriends happened to see it going down and jumped on him. They beat the shit out of him. The cops arrested him while he was in the hospital."

"Serves him right."

"That's the thing. He was never read his rights, so anything he said was inadmissible, and he said plenty."

"It seems the guy knows his stuff."

"His father was a criminal lawyer. Allen went to Yale himself. He quit after three years."

"My alma mater," I said.

"It happens that a college girl disappeared while he was attending school there. She was never seen again either. And guess what? They were dating."

I thought back to Susie and how her father abused and used her as a young girl and then finally murdered her. I wanted to get Dallas bad.

"Jesus," I said. "What do the cops need to get this guy?"

"He has to be caught in the act, or they find a girl at his home I guess," Ron said. "Maybe a body."

"Would you mind putting a tail on him for a while?" I asked.

"It would be my pleasure. I'd love to be the one to get this guy."

The next day I already had my schedule cleared. Malinda and I were taking Diane to the beach. We packed a picnic and picked her up at eleven.

It was another beautiful, hot, humid day in paradise. We laid our towels out on the sand and sat facing the water.

Diane pulled off her shorts and t-shirt to reveal a skimpy bikini. I looked at Malinda. She smiled at me reassuringly.

"I love it here," Diane said. "Everything is so beautiful."

I noticed a few of the local boys watching Diane. I didn't like it, but she was beautiful and coming of age.

She smiled at them. That was all it took. The next thing I knew three skinny boys ran circles around us while throwing a Frisbee to each other.

The Frisbee kept coming closer until Diane reached out and caught it. This was an invitation for the boys to come closer.

She tossed it to one of them.

"Thanks," he said. "You wanna play?"

Diane looked at me.

No, God. Please don't make me make this decision. Malinda looked at me also.

"Go ahead," I said. "But stay right here."

"Thanks, Cam," she said as she jumped up.

The game didn't last very long before they all huddled around and just talked. The boys flexed inconspicuously, obviously hoping Diane would see how strong they were. Diane tilted her head and posed occasionally. I hated it.

After a few minutes, she waved to them and returned to her towel next to us.

"Are they from your school?" I asked.

"Yeah, I've seen them around. The one with the long black hair is Johnny Decker; he's been in my class since the first grade."

I didn't know of anything else to say so I kept quiet. In a few minutes, Diane looked at me and smiled.

"I'm waiting for a man like you, Cam. There aren't too many around."

"They don't get to be like Cam until they get old," Malinda said.

"Then I'll wait."

We laughed.

"I want to go to college to be a psychiatrist," Diane said out of the blue. "By the time I get my degree, the men will be old enough."

"A psychiatrist?" I asked. "That's the first I heard of that."

"I figure Key West could use a good one," she said.

"You're right about that."

This little girl was an old soul. I hoped she wouldn't skip her childhood wanting to grow up too quickly.

We finished the day with an ice cream from the beach bar. It was melting so fast we ended up licking some of it off our wrists.

We gathered our towels and basket and walked to the car, Malinda, and Diane both holding my hands. I hoped we would have many more of these days together.

Later, I learned something about that day. Turned out Al Dallas, hiding in the shade of a Royal Palm unbeknownst to me, watched us as we left the beach.

Chapter 4

Ron Stiller kept vigilance on Dallas from a safe distance. He followed him to the grocery store and to the Liquor Mart.

They returned to Al's house. It was a small but clean, well-kept home in the old town area of Key West. *A million plus*, Ron figured. *What's this guy doing selling cocaine on the street? He could have been a lawyer or almost anything else he wanted to be. His father's loaded. Maybe he had an all-consuming need to kill young women and didn't have time to work.*

After waiting two more hours in his car -- and one large soft drink, one snicker bar and one bag of chips later, he saw Al leave his house again. Ron followed him to US 1, where he took it north and turned left onto College Road, arriving at Hodges University just as the classes ended. The parking lot was full of students. Dallas drove back and forth through the lot with seemingly no particular direction in mind. Ron parked at the entrance and watched him.

Dallas pulled over near the exit and shut off his engine. Cars were passing him and leaving the area. Ron saw Dallas adjust his mirror, so he could see behind him without giving himself away. It looked as though he were waiting for someone. Was it another drug deal?

Finally, Dallas started his car. When a young girl in a blue VW passed him, he pulled out behind her. Ron waited until they both passed him and pulled out three cars behind Dallas.

They drove to an apartment complex where the college students shared rooms. The expense of living in Key West was so high that it was the usual practice to share an apartment with four or five other students.

The girl parked her car and walked to the apartment building. After Dallas pulled to the curb close to the entrance, he said something to the girl who waved at him as she entered the building.

Ron managed to get a few pictures of them both.

Dallas waited a few minutes, his eyes on several other girls entering the building. When they were all inside, he started his car and left.

What was he up to? He was definitely stalking these girls. Was he going to grab one of them this close to home? Maybe he just needed to look at them. A little fuel for the fire so to speak.

Ron followed Dallas to the Bare Assets strip bar. *I guess the little school girls got him all fired up,* Ron thought.

Ron decided to go home and find him again the next day. He called me a few hours later.

"Hi Ron, any news?"

Ron relayed the events of the day and filled me in on his most troubling thoughts.

"Okay," I said. "Thanks for doing this for us."

"My pleasure. I think I'll start earlier tomorrow. I feel like he's on the verge of something."

I called Jim and gave him the report.

"We should do something before *he* does," Jim said.

"We can't prove anything yet other than the guy likes to watch young girls."

"I'd like to get a closer look at his house," Jim said.

"We can't do that," I told him.

"Yeah, I know, but we have to do something."

My secretary stepped into my office, "Mr. Dallas is here to see you," she said.

"I'll call you back," I said. "Dallas is here."

I didn't stand to shake his hand this time. Dallas noticed and grinned.

"What can I do for you?" I asked.

"Well, I was at the beach yesterday and saw this beautiful young girl. Then to my surprise, I saw she was with you. I knew she wasn't your wife because she was with you too. Frankly, I already know what your wife looks like." He smiled and licked his lips. "I was wondering if you could introduce me to the girl," he said and smiled again, his mouth going up on one side.

I kept my cool. Life goes on.

"No, I don't think so, Al. She's underage and as your attorney, I don't think it would be a good idea."

"Ah, too bad," he said. "She looks mighty good in a bikini. I could only imagine what she would look like with it off."

"She would look like an underage girl," I said.

I was thinking Dallas was probably wearing a recorder. He wouldn't bait me like this if he weren't.

"Anything else I can do for you?" I said.

"Yeah, change your mind and let me fuck that little girl."

"Gosh Al, I just can't. As I said, she's underage. That would be against the law."

Once again, I thought about how Susie was victimized by older men. Dallas was the same kind of pervert as Mr. Powers and the other lowlife's her father brought around. I wanted to see them all dead. I was pretty sure I was going to see this one die.

"If there's nothing else," I said standing, towering above the seated man, "I have a busy schedule today."

Dallas stood, and I stepped closer to him so I could look down on the shorter man, just to intimidate and we walked to the door. I thought I did a good job of not saying anything that would get the case thrown out of court.

At the door, he reached out to shake my hand. My hand sweated clammily. I couldn't do it. When I reached toward him, I dropped my hand and grabbed his balls. I squeezed as hard as I could.

He dropped to the floor in pain and threw up explosively.

"Are you alright, Al?" I asked.

He couldn't answer. He lay there holding himself, breathing hard and sweating.

"Should I get you some water or something," I asked and kicked him in the stomach.

He threw up again.

"Well, let me know if you need anything," I said and pulled his shirt up.

There was the recorder. I ripped it off, went into the bathroom, took out the tape and flushed it down the toilet.

It was another twenty minutes before he could get to his feet.

"If you ever say another word about her, I'll kill you," I said.

He didn't speak; he just opened the door and hobbled out.

Chapter 5

I called Jim back and told him about our conversation.

"I'll kill him," Jim said.

"Get in line," I said.

"We have to get him for something," Jim said. "If we can just get him in jail, then we can take our time to investigate his past. I'd love to pin one of those murders on him."

"That's already been tried. They couldn't prove anything."

"I'm getting Diane out of town for a few weeks," Jim said.

"Sounds like a good idea," I said.

I really didn't want her here where Dallas could get to her either.

"We can take her to my parents in Maine," Jim said.

"I'll call the airport and have my plane ready to go. I'll meet you there at five."

"They'll be glad to have her," Jim said.

Diane wasn't too thrilled with the prospect of being gone for a few weeks, but she understood, as she always does. She sat in the copilot's seat next to me. She read off the check-off list while I carefully followed, making sure everything was in order.

Once we were in the air and our heading was set, I let her have the controls. She handled the 421C perfectly.

Jim and I stayed the night at the family home with Diane and Jim's parents. Despite his parents being in their eighties, they were still quite active. They were thrilled to have Diane all to themselves. She had a way of making you feel young again.

Ron Stiller was eating breakfast and watching the news the next morning when a reporter, standing in front of the same apartment building Ron had watched Dallas stop in front of two days ago, came on the screen.

The reporter was saying, "Her roommates said she went to her car to get her cell phone. When she didn't return an hour later, they got concerned and called the police." Then they showed a blue VW sitting in the parking lot. Ron was sure it was the same car the girl was driving when Dallas followed her.

They put a picture of the missing girl on the screen and asked that if anyone has any information on her whereabouts to call, and then they put the hotline number on the screen.

That was her. It was the same girl Dallas had followed and talked to at the apartment parking lot.

That son of a bitch had kidnapped her.

My phone rang. "Hello."

"Cam, its Ron. He's taken another girl."

We told Diane we would be back to get her in a few days. I hoped it wouldn't take any longer than that. She hugged us and told us to be careful flying back to Key West.

"Can you handle the plane without me?" she asked.

"I'll do my best," I said.

We met Ron at our office that afternoon. He already had a file folder on the missing girl and pictures of Dallas talking to her from two days ago.

"I went to his house this morning," Ron said. "His car is in the driveway, but there was no sign of life. The house was dark, and the window shades were drawn."

"Do you think he has her in there?" I asked.

"There's a good chance he does."

"Let's go get her," Jim said.

"We can't, but the police can," I said. "Ron, can you call the police from a phone booth and tell them you saw the girl being forced into his house?"

"Yeah, I'll do it. If we're wrong, then it won't really matter. If we're right, it might save her life."

Ron made the call and parked down the street from Al Dallas's house. He waited for almost an hour before a squad car arrived.

Two uniformed police got out and went to the door.

They knocked and waited. There was no answer. They knocked again. Still no answer. One of them pulled a card from his wallet, stuck it in the screen door jamb and they left.

"Are you shitting me," Ron said to himself.

When the police were gone, Ron walked to the house. He went around back and tried to see in the windows. They were covered like the front ones were. He tried the door. It was locked. Standing back, he raised his foot and slammed it into the door. The lock plate shattered, and the door flew open, sending wood splinters flying.

Ron stood back to the left of the door and waited. Nothing happened. He peeked around the corner. The house was dark with no sounds coming from inside.

He reached in, found the light switch and flipped it up. A bare bulb hanging from the ceiling came on and cast a shadowy light on the walls.

Ron entered through the kitchen. He made a quick search of the house and found no one there.

On the kitchen table was a notepad. On the top page was an address in Brunswick, Maine. He ripped the page off and put it in his pocket.

Satisfied no one was there, he left the house, not bothering to close the door.

Ron called me and told me about the police giving up easily and him breaking in the back door.

"So, you didn't find anything that could lead us to him?" I asked.

"No, just an address on a notepad," he said. "I tore it off and kept it. I'll check it out, but it was in Brunswick, Maine, so it probably won't do us any good."

"Brunswick, Maine?" I said. "What's the address?"

"Just a minute," he said and fished the paper from his pocket.

When he read the address to me, I had to sit. My legs were weak.

"That's Jim's parent's house," I said. "Diane's there."

Chapter 6

Jim called his parents' house and got no answer. He called Diane's cell.

"Hi, Dad," she answered. "What's up?"

He was relieved to hear her voice. He slumped in his chair visibly shaken, overcome with relief.

"Just checking on you. How's it going?"

"It's only been six hours, dad. What's the problem?"

Only six hours, he thought. *How am I going to leave her there with that maniac on the loose?*

"Where's Mom and Dad?"

"Grandpa's napping and Gramma's at the store. You sound worried, Dad."

He never could hide anything from Diane. *She'll make a good psychiatrist someday.*

"Okay," he said. "There's a case we're working on, and we found Mom and Dad's address on his notepad. He might be trying to make us think he's after you."

"In other words," she said. "He's after me."

"We don't know, but he knows where you are."

"Isn't that why I'm here in the first place?"

"Yes, it is."

"What's he look like?"

"Sloppy, with a frizzy ponytail. Receding hairline."

"If I see anyone like that, I'll scream."

"I'm sorry I got you into this. I'm coming to be with you tonight," Jim said.

"You don't need to, Dad. I'll be all right and I know your schedule. You have a court case tomorrow."

"I'll put it on hold," he said. "Or let Cam handle it."

I had entered the office and heard the last part.

"Handle what?" I said.

"It's Diane; she's trying to talk me out of going there," he said.

"Give me the phone," I ordered.

"Hey, girl. Everything okay there?" I asked.

"Quit worrying, Cam. We're fine."

"Can't quit," I said. "I'll see you in a few hours."

I handed the phone back to Jim and told him I would go to Maine. He could stay and handle his case. We all agreed.

As soon as we hung up, the phone rang again.

"Jim, it's Ron."

"What's up, Ron?"

"I'm in jail. The police pulled me over a few minutes ago. Dallas has sworn a complaint that I broke into his house."

"Dallas is here?"

"Yeah, it was a set-up. He's going to file for a mistrial because his attorney broke into his house. I told them I don't work for you, but they say they have proof I do."

"I'll show them the file with Dallas and the missing girl. Maybe they'll change their tune then."

"She's not missing. She's here with Dallas. They're dating."

"Crap," Jim said. "We'll be there shortly to get you out."

"Sorry about this," Ron said. "I fell for it all the way."

We were able to get Ron out on bail. Eventually, the judge did end up declaring a mistrial and Al Dallas walked out a free man. The drug charges were dropped.

Al eventually dropped the charges against Ron, but not before he had spent fifty-thousand dollars on lawyers. We, of course, dropped the fees.

One afternoon a week later, I was in Sloppy Joe's having a drink and saw Al Dallas walk in with the college girl. We found out her name was Annie Walker. She was twenty-one.

She had bruises on her cheek and arms. I watched them as they took a seat three tables from mine. Dallas saw me and leered.

"How's Diane?" he said.

He grabbed Annie by the arm and roughly pulled her to him, kissing her hard on the mouth. He then reached out and squeezed her breast. She flinched and tried to push him away. He looked at me again and snickered.

I couldn't do anything about it unless she protested, and he hit her. If I intervened at that point, the courts would be on his side.

An old friend of mine happened to come in; he waved and sat down with me, sliding onto the seat with noticeable agility. Greg Rollins worked out on a regular basis and had the body to prove it.

I pointed to Al and filled Greg in on what all had happened. Greg had a younger sister who was the victim of a gang rape when she was in high school. I figured that was why I could see him turning red. I told him not to do anything – that is as long as I was around.

After a few more drinks, I paid our tab and left. Greg stayed.

Dallas looked at Greg and grinned again, then hit Annie on the side of the head with an open hand. She fell sideways in her chair. Dallas grabbed her arm and pulled her upright.

He enjoyed the show he was putting on and knowing no one could do anything about it. Greg didn't see it that way.

Dallas had gone a little too far this time.

Greg rose and walked to Dallas and Annie.

"Is this man bothering you?" he asked Annie.

She looked up at Greg. Her eyes were glossed over but the bruises on her body and face told the story.

"Get up," Greg told Dallas.

"Fuck you," he said.

Greg pulled Dallas to his feet. Dallas swung his right fist, catching Greg on the jaw. When Greg didn't flinch, Dallas got a worried look on his face.

The ambulance arrived shortly after Greg left. Dallas was taken to the Lower Keys Medical Center. He would remain there for four days.

There were no witnesses at the packed bar. The waitress told the police she saw a man come in and attack Dallas then run away. She said she had never seen him before, even though she did date Greg from time to time.

Annie was admitted to a drug rehab center in Key West where she told them she had been forced to shoot heroin by Allan Dallas.

Once again, the charges were dropped when a search of Dallas's property failed to turn up any drugs. Dallas's new attorney found evidence showing this wasn't Annie's first relationship with drugs.

A month later, I took it upon myself to follow Dallas again. His routine hadn't changed much. He still hung out in the college parking lot and would follow girls back to their apartments.

On the second day, I saw Annie. She was back with her friends and seemed to be doing okay. She was laughing, and a young man was flirting with her. *Good for her,* I thought.

I saw Dallas pull to the curb and watch her before he finally got out of his car and walked to the couple. They spoke, and Dallas pushed the kid she was talking with. Though he stumbled, he didn't fall.

He pushed Dallas back and a fight ensued. I smiled as Dallas got his ass kicked. The kid was thin, but he was like a tornado of fists and kicks. Finally, when Dallas quit fighting back, the couple walked away. Dallas got to his feet and lurched back to his car.

When he drove to the other end of the lot and parked again, I watched him curiously, believing he was waiting for the boy to return.

When the kid did finally come back out of the apartment and get in his car, Dallas followed him.

I followed Dallas.

Dallas wasn't good at hiding when it came to tailing someone. The kid spotted him right away and turned onto a side street. Dallas did also. I stayed a block back.

The boy got out and went to Dallas's car, opened the door and dragged him out. He beat him again. This time when the boy walked away, Dallas didn't get up.

What an idiot.

A passerby stopped when he saw Dallas lying in the street. The man got out of his car and helped him up. After the stranger left, Dallas drove back toward his place.

I drove away smiling. It was a good day.

Chapter 7

Diane had returned home, and things were normal again for the most part. I couldn't get Dallas out of my mind, so I still followed him a few days a week. I found out Ron was doing the same. He didn't take kindly to being set up by Dallas.

Diane was walking home from school when a car matching Dallas's pulled over in front of her. She was near a B&B and ran inside. She was a smart girl and knew not to take any chances. The car sped away, but not before the woman working at the front desk got the license plate number.

Diane gave me the number. When I ran it, I found it was registered to Allen Dallas. I told the police, but of course, there was nothing they could do. Nothing actually happened.

I received a call from the Key West police department a few days later. Annie Walker was missing again; her friends hadn't seen her for three days. She hadn't shown up for any of her classes and her parents had no idea where she was.

I called Ron. He happened to be watching Dallas's house at the time.

"He just pulled into his driveway," Ron said. "He's been acting differently for the last few days. He doesn't go out much and the curtains are closed tight."

"You think he has her in there?" I asked.

"He might. He's just crazy enough to do it again."

I'll check back with you in a few hours," I said. "If you see anything, call me."

Jim came into the office. "What was that about?" he asked.

"Annie's missing again," I said.

"That son of a bitch, I bet he has her. This time he won't let her go," Jim said. "He tried to get Diane. It's time to end this," and stormed into his office.

Now I had to worry about what he might do.

Jim sat at his desk, getting more furious. The more he thought about it, the more he knew he had to put an end to it. He snuck out of the office and got in his car, driving toward Dallas's house.

Ron watched Dallas pull his car out of the driveway. He turned it around and backed it in all the way to the rear of the house.

What the fuck is he doing? Ron thought.

When Dallas had gone back into his house, Ron saw Jim pull to the curb in front.

My phone rang again.

"Did you know Jim was here?" Ron said.

"No, I had no idea. I thought he went back to his office. What's he doing?"

"He's just sitting in his car."

"I'm on my way."

Ron watched Jim, who was watching the house.

"Don't do anything crazy," Ron whispered.

Ron leaned down and removed his gun from beneath the seat. He checked the chamber to make sure it was fully loaded. When he looked back up, Jim's car door was open, and he was gone.

"Shit," Ron said.

Jim kicked the back door to Al's house. It flew open and he entered. Annie lay on the floor, bound with duct tape. Dallas stood over her holding a gun. Pointed at Jim.

"You son of a bitch," Jim said.

Dallas just grinned, keeping the gun aimed at Jim.

"What the hell do you think you're doing?" Jim asked.

"So, Cam Derringer and you thought you would take the law into your own hands."

Jim looked at the girl. She was moving.

"She ain't dead – yet," he said.

"Let her go," Jim said.

"I will, but I need some money first," answered Dallas. "I was just going to leave

Key West when I realized I was broke. Now a cash cow has landed in my lap."

"I'm not giving you a plug nickel," Jim spat.

"If you don't, I'll kill you both. Her first."

"Just leave 'er and go," Jim said.

"We had us some fun last night," Dallas said and laughed.

Jim lunged toward Dallas but was too slow. Dallas swung the gun around and hit him on the chin. He went down and lay on the floor next to the girl.

Dallas picked up a pen and notepad from the kitchen table, wrote down an account number and told Jim to empty his bank account into it. "I swear I'll kill her if you don't do it right now."

He handed Jim a cell phone, "Call em' now!"

Jim relented. He transferred five million dollars to the account leaving only sixty-five thousand in his own.

"Thank you, sir," Dallas said wadding up the number and eating it. "Now get up and help me load her in the trunk."

"Fuck you Dallas. You leave her here with me."

"I'm not finished with her yet," he said pointing the gun at Jim. "You going to help me?"

"No way," Jim said.

"I'll kill ya," he said.

Jim lunged at Dallas again. Dallas pulled the trigger. The bullet caught Jim in the forehead, and he died instantly.

I was on my way to Dallas's house when Ron called me again.

"Jim's disappeared, and I think I heard a gunshot," Ron said already out of the car and running toward the house.

"I'm almost there," I said.

Dallas picked the girl up and carried her out the back door. He raised the trunk of his car and placed her inside.

"Hold it right there," Ron said running toward Dallas.

Dallas answered with a shot, which hit Ron in the shoulder.

Ron went down.

Finally arriving at Dallas's house, I saw the car trunk open and Ron on the ground. I flew into the driveway ramming Dallas's car.

The force knocked Dallas to the ground. It also stunned me for an instant. When I regained my senses, I saw Dallas getting up and raising a gun toward me. I opened the car door and ducked down beside it, pulling my own gun from my belt.

We exchanged a few shots going wide at either end.

"Give it up, Dallas. The police are on their way," I shouted.

His answer was another volley of gunfire.

"I'll kill this little girl like I did your buddy in there if you don't back off," he said. "Or I'll trade her for the little one you had at the beach. She would be really fun."

My heart sank. Was Jim dead? Did he really kill him?

My anger took over and I stood and ran toward Dallas shooting as I went. He returned fire. A bullet caught me in the leg, but I kept going. I finally saw one of my rounds hit him in the chest. He went down.

When I stopped beside him, he still had his gun in his hand. He raised it toward me. I fired one more bullet right between his eyes.

Jim was dead. Now I had to break the news to Diane. For the second time in as many years, Diane would be grieving the loss of her parent.

Her inheritance was gone. We never found Jim's money. We didn't tell her about the money, but somehow, she knew. The courts granted Malinda and me legal guardianship of Diane.

As for me, I was disbarred for my role in Jim's death. I applied for and received my Private Investigators license. I've managed to eke out a living at it. We were able to keep our boat, a forty-two-foot Meridian Sedan, and our house.

Chapter 8

It was evident that Diane was in a state of depression. I called a friend, Richard Serletic, who has a psychiatric practice in Key West.

"Hi Cam," he answered his phone.

"How are you, Richard?" I asked.

"I'm doing good, but you must not be. You haven't called me for a few months."

"I know. Malinda and I have been trying to deal with everything that's going on ourselves. But now I think I could use some help."

"Diane?" he said.

"Yes, I'm afraid so. She's going through a depression. I don't know what to do other than hold her."

"Bring her in tomorrow if you can. I'll be glad to talk to her. Sometimes it has to be someone who isn't so close to the person."

"Thanks, Richard."

We made an appointment for the next day. Now I had to get Diane to agree to it.

I discovered that was the easy part. She readily agreed to go see him. She said it would be good practice for when she would be a psychiatrist.

That night we sat on the lanai and ate grilled hamburgers. Diane said she was excited about meeting with Richard tomorrow. While that should be a good thing, it didn't seem quite right. She didn't say anything about getting help. She was more eager to learn the so-called, 'tricks of the trade' than she was to get help.

"Diane," I said, "you know you're going to see Richard, so you can talk about your mom and dad, don't you?"

She bowed her head slightly. "Yeah Cam, I know. I'm trying to deal with it. I really am, but I miss them so much."

She started to cry. Then she came to me and sat on my lap hugging me. She buried her head in my shoulder and sobbed.

I looked at Malinda who was also crying. I knew we had a long road ahead of us. I just didn't know how bad things could really get.

When we entered Richard's office the next day, Diane shook his hand and said it was nice to see him again. They had met a few years earlier at one of Diane's baseball games. Richard had a granddaughter Diane's age.

"Okay, Cam," Richard said, "I'll see you in about an hour."

He was excusing me.

I hugged Diane and kissed her.

"See ya in a bit."

"I'm fine, Cam," she said making a shooing motion with her hands.

I sat in the parking lot for an hour, just in case. When I saw Diane walk out, I pulled the car to the curb. She got in but didn't say anything.

"You alright, honey?

She stared at me for a few seconds and said, "I'll never see them again."

"I believe you will, someday. I believe we'll all be united again in Heaven."

"Yeah, maybe," she said softly.

The drive home was quiet. Maybe it was a bad idea to take her to talk about it. Maybe she just wasn't ready.

When we entered the house, Diane ran to her bedroom and closed the door. I told Malinda about our conversation and how I thought it might not be time yet.

An hour later, Diane came out of her room dressed in cut-off shorts and a halter top.

"Can I go down to Duvall Street? Some of the kids are meeting for lunch at the hot dog stand," she said excitedly.

Malinda and I exchanged a quick, involuntary glance. This was a sudden change in mood for Diane.

"Sure," I said before I had a chance to think it over.

"Thanks," she said over her shoulder, running back to her room.

She reappeared a few moments later with her backpack over her shoulder. She kissed Malinda and then me.

"Do you need a ride?" I asked.

"No thanks," she said.

Before I could regain my senses, she was out the door.

"Wow," Malinda said. "What was that?"

"I don't know, but it's a one-eighty from an hour ago."

I went to the front door and opened it in time to see Diane get in a car with a boy. They were gone before I could protest.

"I don't like it," Malinda said.

"Neither do I, but we have to give her some space. She's going through a lot. I'll give her a call in a couple of hours."

Exactly two hours later, I called Diane's cell phone.

"Hey, Cam," she answered.

"Hi honey, I'm just checking on you. Everything alright?"

"I can't believe you waited two hours. You must be growing up," she joked.

"We all have to sometime," I said trying to sound like I wasn't worried.

"We're good here," she said. "Just sitting on the beach talking."

"Who's with you?"

"Cam, you *are* worried," she said and giggled.

"I can't help it."

"Well, Lisa, Ronda, Tammy, Barry, and Jamie. We're behaving."

"Okay," I said. "Call me when you're ready to come home and I'll come to get you."

"I have a ride. I'll see you in a few hours," she said. "Bye."

The line went dead. I didn't feel any better now that I had talked to her. She sounded okay but maybe a little distant, from me anyway.

Another hour passed, and I was walking the floor. I don't make a good dad. I worry too much.

"Cam, why don't you go play golf or something," Malinda said. "I'll be here, and I'll call you as soon as I hear from her."

I was thinking it over when the house phone rang.

I jumped on it. "Hello."

"Hi. Is Diane home?"

"No, she isn't. She should be home any time though," I said to make myself feel better. "Would you like for her to call you?"

"Yeah, if you don't mind. This is Lisa. Sorry to call your house but she didn't answer her cell."

"Lisa? Were you at the beach with her today?"

Lisa hesitated.

"Lisa?"

"Well, she was supposed to meet all of us today, but she never showed up," she said.

My heart was in my throat.

"She didn't show up?" I heard myself say.

"No, sir."

I thought for a moment. "Do you know a boy with a blue Camaro?"

Silence again.

"Lisa, this is important," I said.

"I don't know him, but he's been hanging around school lately with some of the other guys. He's been talking to Diane a lot."

"Do you know where he lives?" I said hearing panic in my voice.

"No, I'm sorry."

"Will you ask around for me? Call me if you hear from her."

“I will,” she said. “She’ll be okay. Diane’s a smart girl. She won’t do anything she shouldn’t do.”

“She already has,” I said. “Call me.”

.

Chapter 9

"Who were the other friends she was with?" I asked Malinda.

"You know them, Cam. It was Tammy, Ronda, Jamie, and Barry."

"Barry who?" I said.

"Barry Phillips. You met him at her school play. Remember, his mother is the tall Brunette in the halter top and the mini skirt," Malinda said.

"Oh yeah," I said and then thought I should have said, "No, I don't recall her." It was too late, but Malinda let it go.

I called Lisa back and got the phone numbers from her.

First, I called Barry. Not because of his mother, but because his name was on top of the list. His mother answered.

"Mrs. Phillips," I said. "This is Cam Derringer. Diane's father."

"Hi, Cam. I know who you are. Whadda ya want?"

She had a very seductive voice and was using it for all it was worth.

"Well," I said, "I'm trying to find Diane and I think she was with Barry and some friends at the beach today."

"He's not home yet," she said softly. "But you can come over and look for her."

"Thanks, I'll try the other kids first."

"Okay, if you don't have any luck, I'll be here."

I hung up. Malinda was looking at me.

"Barry's not home yet," I said.

She laughed, "What else did she say?"

"She said I could come to look for Diane."

"I better keep an eye on you."

I called Tammy on her cell phone.

"Hi mister Derringer," she said.

"Hi, Tammy. Is Diane with you?"

I waited for her to say, "Oh yeah, you want to talk to her?" but what I heard was, "No we haven't seen her today. She was going to meet us here at the hotdog stand."

"Do you know the boy's name who drives a blue Camaro?"

"I think it's John or something like that. I told Diane not to talk to him, he's creepy."

"How old is this kid?"

"He looks to me to be around twenty-five or so."

"Have you seen him today?"

"No. Is Diane okay?" she questioned nervously.

"I hope so. I saw her leave with him. She said she was going to meet you guys."

"She was," Tammy said.

"Okay, thanks. If you see her will you tell her to call me?"

"I will mister Derringer. Call me too if *you* hear from her," she said with urgency in her voice.

"Okay Tammy, Bye."

"What do ya think, Cam?" Malinda said.

"I think he was waiting for her to come outside, and when she did, he said he'd give her a ride. Now she's lying to me and is with him somewhere. She's fifteen and he's twenty-five. I'll beat him to death if he touches her."

"Just calm down, Cam. We'll find her," Malinda said. "Diane has a good head on her shoulders."

"Yeah, but she's no match for an older guy. I've been through this twice already. Both times ended in tragedy."

"Not this time, Cam. We'll bring her home safe," she said grabbing her keys. "Come on, I'll drive."

We drove around town aimlessly. I called Sheriff Buck and told him what was going on.

"It's too early to file a missing person. You know that."

"Yeah, but this is like kidnapping."

"Not really," he said. "Bad judgment? Yeah."

"She's fifteen, he's around twenty-five," I yelled into the phone.

"Calm down, Cam. I didn't say I wouldn't look for 'er. I just said it's too early for legal papers."

I sat silent.

"I'll put an APB out on the blue Camaro," Buck said. "We can't pull over every one of them, but I'll have the officers eyeball the passengers. I'll call Strickland at the city police office and ask him to do the same."

"Thanks, Willie. I owe you one."

"My thanks will be getting Diane home safe."

We drove around for another hour. No sign of her, so we returned home hoping to find her.

When she wasn't there, my panic subsided and my training as a PI went into full throttle.

I pulled up all the blue Camaro's that were licensed in Florida in Dade, Broward and Collier Counties. I came up with over three hundred. I then entered the first name Johnathon, John, and Johnny. Now it was fifteen.

I started in on the ages, manually. I came up with five under the age of thirty.

I checked the addresses and found two within fifty miles. One here in Key West, John Drake and one in Marathon Key, John Barnette.

"I'll be back in a few minutes," I told Malinda. "You stay here in case she comes home."

"Where are you going?"

"To White Street to see John and his blue Camaro."

I knocked on the door at 2301 White Street. It was answered by a young man in his late twenties. Twenty-six to be exact.

"John Drake?" I asked.

"Who wants to know?" he said defensively.

"Cam Derringer. I'm Diane's father."

"Who's Diane?"

"The girl you had in your car today. Remember, the one who's only fifteen," I said, my voice rising.

"I don't know what you're talking about, mister. I haven't been with any fifteen-year-old girls."

Another voice came from behind him, that of a young woman. "What's he want, Johnny?"

"I'm not sure. I think his daughter."

The girl appeared at the door. She was a small blonde-haired girl with a tattoo on her shoulder.

"We've been here all day, sir. I haven't seen your daughter. Why would you think she was here?" she asked.

"I saw her get into a blue Camaro, like the one in your driveway, with a boy in his twenties," I said.

"It wasn't Johnny. He's been with me all day."

"Mister Derringer," Johnny said, "It's none of my business, but there are a lot of blue Camaros in Key West."

"The boy's name was John," I said.

"Sorry, I don't know another John with a car like mine."

I looked over their shoulders into their house.

"She's not here," the girl said.

"Wait a minute," John said and disappeared into the house.

He reappeared with a pistol in his hand.

"Come on in and take a look," he said and held the door open.

I knew I shouldn't, but I did. After touring the house, I apologized and went back to the porch.

"Don't worry about it," he said. "I hope you find her."

"Thanks," I said and apologized again and left.

When I was on my way home, my cell rang.

"Hello."

"Cam," the male voice said.

I recognized it right away.

"Sunny, how are you?"

It was Sunny Ray, a friend who lives in Marathon Key. He's a country singer with fifteen platinum albums to his name. He owns an island off the Key called Rum City Bar.

"This is a nice surprise. I haven't seen you for a few months," I said.

"I've been on a small tour," he said. "It's always something."

"Yeah, I guess."

"The reason I called you is, I swear I saw Diane at Sombrero Beach today. Is she here?"

"She might be," I said excitedly. "She disappeared today. I've been everywhere looking for her."

"She was with a guy and another couple. They were in their car and gone before I could get to her."

"A blue Camaro?" I asked.

"Yeah, it was."

"Did she look as if she was with them willingly?"

"It appeared that way, but Cam, that guy was too old for her and he had a beer in his hand."

Chapter 10

"I'm on my way there," I said. "I'll be there in about an hour."

"I'm gonna go look for the car. Call me when you get here."

"I have a possible address," I said and read it to him.

"I'll check it out."

I called Malinda and told her what I was doing.

"Cam, you're not thinking," she said. "The car that was here might have been licensed by someone else. Maybe it's John's dad's car. He could live anywhere."

"Sunny saw her in Marathon," I said.

"He did?"

"Yes, and the guy she was with was drinking."

"Find them and let the police handle it, Cam. That's what they do," Malinda pleaded.

"I'll play it by ear," I said. I had no intentions of letting the police handle it.

Sunny called a few minutes later.

"I'm at the house. The car isn't here."

"Marathon isn't that big. We'll find her somewhere."

"I'm gonna start at the north end of town and at Key Colony. When you come into town start at the Sunset Bar and work this way," Sunny said.

"Will do," I said.

I hadn't heard from Sunny by the time I got to Marathon. I pulled into the parking lot of the Sunset Bar and drove up and down every aisle. There was no blue Camaro here.

I pulled back out onto Highway One and followed it north to the 7 Mile Grill. A blue Camaro was in the parking lot. I called Sunny.

"I think I might have 'em," I said. "7 Mile Grill."

"I'll be there in five minutes. Don't go in yet. They'll be okay there."

"Hurry."

Diane and John finished their meal and walked next door to the Sea Dog Charters Marina, leaving their car at the grill.

"There it is," John said pointing to a twenty-two-foot Sea Ray sitting at the dock. "They have her fueled up and ready to go."

"I don't think I should," Diane said, worried and confused. "I want to go back home."

"Come on. You're a big girl. We'll go out for an hour and have a few more beers, then I'll take you home."

Diane already felt tipsy from the two beers she had consumed. This was the first time she'd had any alcohol and she didn't like the way it made her feel.

John took her hand and led her to the boat.

"Here ya go," he said and lifted her in.

Diane slid into the seat and leaned back. She had no willpower now, things were starting to get blurry. She was getting sleepy and couldn't hold her eyes open.

John pushed the boat away from the dock, looked down at Diane and smiled. *The Rohypnol is kicking in. By the time we anchor in the cove, she'll be out cold.*

I stood beside my car and watched the grill. I wanted to go inside but I would wait for Sunny. I might overreact as I usually do, but if I do it in front of witnesses, it could be big trouble.

I looked down the road for Sunny's old truck. I glanced at the marina next door and watched a boat pulling away from the dock.

The guy was standing behind the wheel and a blonde girl was slumped in the back seat of the boat. I studied the scene more intensely. *Is that Diane? I think so.*

Sunny pulled into the lot. I ran past his truck, motioning for him to follow me. When we reached the marina, I pointed at the boat and said, "That's them."

Sunny ran inside and returned with the key to a boat.

"Come on," he said.

We climbed into a twenty-foot Baha. Sunny fired it up while I untied the lines. I pushed us off and we accelerated away from the dock. We were leaving a heavy wake through the no wake zone. I'd deal with that later.

"Do you see 'em?" I yelled.

"Not yet, but they couldn't be too far ahead of us."

We could see to our right. There were no boats, so we went straight out into the Knights Channel.

"There's a cove on the other side of the key here," Sunny said. "We'll check that out. If they were out in the open water, we'd see 'em."

We saw a boat anchored near the cove, but it looked as if no one was in it. As we approached it, a man's head popped up. When he saw us, he jumped behind the wheel and started the boat. Instead of pulling his anchor in, he threw the line over the side and sped away.

Sunny pushed the throttle all the way forward and we followed the boat. The Sea Ray was gradually putting more distance between him and us.

"We can't catch him," Sunny yelled over his shoulder. "But he can't lose us either."

I knew Diane had to be lying on the floor of the speeding boat. She would be getting beat up pretty bad from the constant bouncing over the waves.

We were headed toward Pigeon Key, a walker's destination from Marathon on the Florida Keys Overseas Heritage Trail.

There was nothing there and nowhere for him to escape to, so why was he going there?

When he got closer to the island his boat slowed. He left the wheel and was fumbling with something in the boat.

Then he stood. He had Diane in his arms. She was naked except for an orange life vest. He tossed her over the side near the key and sped away. We arrived about forty-five seconds later. As Sunny slowed the boat near her, I dove in the water, put my arm around her and swam to the beach.

Sunny pulled the boat to the beach and jumped out.

"Is she okay?" he said.

"She's unconscious. I think she's been drugged. She's breathing okay."

Diane opened her eyes for a few seconds, gave me a weak smile and closed them again. I carried her to the boat and we started back for the marina.

"He got away," Sunny said. "But I know where he lives."

I took the vest off Diane and pulled my t-shirt over her head. It was large enough to cover her body.

"If he raped her, he's dead," I told Sunny.

He just nodded his head.

At the hospital, they did a toxicology test on Diane and found Rohypnol, the date rape drug, in her system.

When she woke, Sunny and I were both standing next to her bed.

"Hi baby," I said. "How ya feeling?"

"Horrible," she said. "I have a headache."

"The doctor gave you something to make you feel better. It'll kick in shortly."

"What happened to me?"

"Your boyfriend drugged you," I said.

"I'm sorry, Cam." She started to cry.

"It'll be okay, Diane. We're going home in a while."

"Hi, Diane," Sunny said.

Diane looked at him. “Sunny, I didn’t see you.”

She reached out her arms. He hugged her.

She was a big Sunny Ray fan and liked to brag to her girlfriends about how he was her good friend.

“Will the two of you excuse me for a minute,” I said. “I need to call Malinda.”

I stepped into the hallway to call. The doctor approached me.

“The exam showed she wasn’t penetrated, but it sounds like you got there just in time.”

“I wish I had been about ten minutes earlier.

“Officer Williams is waiting in the lobby to talk with you,” the doctor said.

“I’ll see him after I make a call. Thanks for your help.”

“You’re welcome. Diane should be able to go home in a few hours.”

I called Malinda and filled her in. She was relieved that I’d found Diane and she wasn’t seriously injured.

Sergeant Williams introduced himself and asked how Diane was doing.

"She's okay for now," I said. "This will probably prove to be a pretty traumatic event. She's lost both of her parents in the last year and now this."

"So, you're not her father?"

"I'm her legal guardian," I said. "I've known her all her life.

To me, she is my daughter."

"Do you know the young man she was with?"

"No. I only found out about him today."

"Do you know where he lives?"

"No sir," I said. I wasn't really lying. I didn't know.

"Do you know his name?" he asked.

"John," I said.

I didn't want the police to pick him up before I had a chance to "Talk" with him.

"Okay," the sergeant said. "I guess I had better talk to Diane. She probably knows the boy's name."

"I don't think she's coherent enough yet," I said.

"I'll wait," he said.

We stood there for a few minutes not saying anything.

"Has Diane ever done anything like this before?" Williams asked.

"No," I said defensively. "She's a good girl. I think she has some issues to deal with from losing her parents."

"Has she had any counseling?"

"She just started seeing a therapist," I said.

"Do you know where she met this boy?"

"Her friend said he's been hanging around school talking to Diane."

"Her friend?"

"Yes, one of her girlfriends. I called her when Diane didn't come home."

"Can I have her name?"

"Tammy Crane."

"You have her number?"

I gave it to him.

He stood in the hall with me for a few more minutes looking over his notes.

Sunny came out of Diane's room and joined us.

"Hi Sunny," Williams said.

"Hey, Jim. You get this case?"

"Yeah, I didn't know you were a part of it."

"Helping out an old friend," Sunny said.

"Mind if I talk with you privately for a minute?" he said to Sunny.

Sunny looked at me.

"It's fine, Sunny," I said.

"Okay. They're getting her release papers ready."

"Thanks," I said.

Sunny returned five minutes later.

"How'd it go?" I asked.

"Okay. He wanted to know if you were a good father."

"Am I?"

"I said you were."

"Sometimes I wonder."

"Don't blame yourself for this, Cam. It's not your fault and if you weren't such a good father, it would have been a lot worse."

Chapter 11

Diane came out in a wheelchair dressed in a hospital gown.

"You look stunning," I said.

"It's really not my color."

Sunny took over the chair from the nurse and we wheeled her to the front lobby where he waited with her while I got the car.

"Let's stop by Rose's house first," Sunny said. "I called her, and she said she can give Diane something to wear."

Rose was Sunny's, first true love. He met her in Evansville, Indiana where she was dancing–on stage.

Sunny was only seventeen, but he and some friends snuck into the Landing strip club. When Rose came on stage, Sunny fell in love. They had a brief love affair for four months before she left town. He discovered her again down here in Marathon when he visited a good friend, Curt James. Rose was married to Curt's father. Awkward.

They've all become good friends now, and Sunny stays with them sometimes when the weather doesn't permit him to take a boat to his island.

In the car, Diane opened up to us. She didn't know why she got in the car with John in the first place.

"I knew better. Then when I talked to you, I felt like I had to prove to the others that I was grown-up and could do as I pleased."

"You don't say."

"I guess I proved otherwise. I played right into his hands."

"Did he hurt you?" I asked.

"No, thanks to you and Sunny. I think he would have."

"Yes, he definitely would have," Sunny said.

"He drugged me, didn't he?"

"Yes," I said.

"Was he going to rape me?"

"I think that was the plan. He already had your clothes off. He put a life jacket on you and threw you into the ocean. That's how he got away from us."

Diane turned red. "The two of you saw me naked?"

"We didn't have much choice," Sunny said.

"If I see him again, I'll kill him," she said angerly.

"No," I said sternly. "We'll let the police handle him."

A few moments of silence followed.

"Sunny, would you sign my hospital gown?" she said.

"Sure will, honey," he said.

I was worried that Diane wasn't taking what happened to her seriously enough. Then I remembered the doctor saying her memory would come and go for a few hours.

Rose met us in the driveway. Diane got out of the car, ran to her and hugged her.

Rose is a beautiful red-haired, green-eyed, five-foot three-inch package of dynamite. I can see how Sunny fell in love with her.

"Hi, Cam," she said and hugged me.

"Rose, it's good to see you again."

"Well, little girl," Rose said, "we need to get you something to wear."

Rose and Diane disappeared into the house. This gave me an opportunity to talk to Sunny.

"I'm going to be gone for a few minutes," I said. "Will you watch Diane until I return?"

"You're not going anywhere without me," Sunny said. "I can't trust you. You'll end up in more trouble than you bargained for."

"Okay, you can go with me but stay out of it."

"We'll see," Sunny said.

Sunny went in to tell Rose we'd be gone for a few minutes. I got in my car and left. I thought I could get to John's house before Sunny caught me.

It was a well-maintained two-story house on the water. Not at all what I expected. The blue Camaro was in the driveway.

I knocked on the door. There was no answer. It was silent inside.

"*John*," I yelled.

No answer.

I knocked again.

Nothing, then I saw the curtain move slightly.

I stepped back and using my foot, I hit the door hard enough to break the lock and the door swung open.

I stepped in and was hit with a club of some kind. My left shoulder took the brunt of the hit and a pain ran down my arm.

I regained my stance quickly and moved to the right staying upright.

John was swinging what I knew now was a fire iron, at me again. I dodged in time and managed to hit him in the jaw with a hard right fist.

The iron fell to the floor and he with it.

I pulled him to his feet by his shirt and punched him hard in the stomach. He doubled over, and I hit him again, this time on the left jaw.

I pulled him up and held him against the wall.

"Hi, big guy," I said. "I'm Diane's father."

"No, you're not," he managed to say between shallow breaths. "Her father's dead. I saw the article in the paper."

I thought for a moment. "Is that what you do, big man? You prey on vulnerable little girls?"

He managed a sneer.

I hit him hard in the nose and felt it break. I let him go and he slid to the floor. I knelt down next to him and said, "I hope you don't think you're a man."

"Fuck you," he said, his eyes watering and blood running from his bent nose.

I hit him again and then again. I would have killed him if Sunny hadn't come through the door and pulled me off of him.

"Cam, stop, you can't do this! I called the police. They're on the way. Let them take care of him."

I sat back on the floor and leaned against the wall. I stared at John and remembered how I killed Susan's father and the way I killed Dallas for raping that young girl. I knew I had to stop.

An ambulance took John away. I was questioned and released by Sergeant Williams.

"We're going to have to speak with you again, Cam," he said.

"Yeah, any time," I said.

We went to the emergency room where we discovered my arm was badly bruised from the hit I took from the fire iron.

Sunny drove me back to Rose's house. I cleaned the blood off my clothes the best I could and removed the sling. I didn't want Diane to see it.

Diane appeared in a pair of Rose's shorts and a t-shirt.

"I offered her a beautiful dress, but this is what she chose," Rose said.

"Well, I think she looks great," I said.

"Yes, you do, Diane," Sunny said and hugged her.

She beamed.

"Let's go," I said. "Malinda's waiting for us."

Diane reached down into a paper sack and pulled out her hospital gown. Handing it to Sunny she said, "You said you'd sign it."

Sunny went to a drawer and got a sharpie. He wrote, '*To my favorite girl in all the world, Sunny Ray.*'

Chapter 12

Malinda was waiting for us when we arrived. She had Diane's bed turned down and some ice-cream sitting out to melt. Diane liked it a little soft.

"Are you okay, Diane?" Malinda asked.

"Yeah," she said and pulled the gown from the paper sack. "Check it out," she said grinning from ear to ear.

Malinda and I exchanged a fleeting glance. Diane needs to accept what has happened in her life. At this point, she seems to be avoiding reality.

Malinda and I kept Diane in therapy for the next two years. She eventually accepted all that has happened.

I always feel like the child when I'm with Diane.

After graduation, we sent her to Yale. She said, "If it was good enough for you, it's good enough for me."

When she graduated, she was offered a position at Yale-New Haven Psychiatric Hospital. Which she turned down.

She said, "There are a lot of people in Key West that need my help."

When Diane returned from school, she was ready to conquer the world. She worked at The Lower Keys Medical Center in Key West for a year as a Psychiatrist before going out on her own. She started building a good clientele. She was right, Key West needed another good psychiatrist.

She told me – life goes on.

I knew she was going to survive.

There was a rash of piracy going down around Key West. I was hired to look into it by a client who had his boat stolen. The boat was found a month later just floating ten miles off the southeastern coast of Miami.

My job was impossible, I knew that. I would never find who was stealing the boats. I did discover they were being used to run drugs. I also realized that several of the owners of the boats were on the verge of bankruptcy. That raised a red flag. It sounded like there was also insurance fraud mixed in with the drug trade.

One morning Malinda took our 42-foot Meridian to Miami to pick up her girlfriends as she had done many times before. They were going to the Bahamas for a week.

"Have you got everything?" I asked her.

"I don't need much," she said. "Just some clothes and a case of wine."

"Love you. Have fun," I said.

I kissed her goodbye and watched her expertly pull the Meridian out of the marina.

She never arrived in Miami. We searched for her but there was no trace.

A month later, we found the boat in the Bahamas in a boatyard. The registration numbers had been changed.

Diane grieved the loss of Malinda as much as I did. Now it was my turn to be strong once more. I promised Diane and myself I would find the men responsible for her disappearance.

Jack Stiller was my new partner. He's Ron's son. He's six-foot-five-inches tall and made of muscle. He's forty-three years old.

I made one rule for Jack the first day he showed up on the job: Diane is off-limits.

He promised that wouldn't be a problem, but I knew it would. Jack has a bit of a checkered past with the women. Diane is my everything now, and I would kill for her.

I spent all my time and resources searching for the men who–I didn't want to say it aloud, but in my heart, I knew–killed Malinda.

Eventually, I lost my house. Before it was foreclosed on, I managed to sell it and buy a houseboat, which I kept docked in Key West. I also lost my airplane. That really hurt.

I was sitting on my new lanai staring at the water when I heard the gate at the end of the dock squeak. I turned and looked. It was Diane. My day brightened.

“Hey, Cam,” she said.

“Hey, Diane. What’s in the sack?” I said looking at a white bag she was holding.

“I brought you something you use to get me all the time. I haven’t had one in years,” she said.

I thought. “No,” I said. “You have chocolate covered honey-buns in there?”

“Yep,” she said beaming. “Betty’s Bakery.”

“I’ll get the milk,” I said.

We sat on the fantail and ate our rolls and talked about all the problems the world had. Things just aren’t the way they used to be.

“Did you get a load of the two girls moving into the first houseboat on the right?” she asked.

“No, I didn’t see them,” I said and then smiled.

“Sure,” she said. “I’m surprised you’re not helping them.”

“I thought I would introduce myself when the work is finished,” I said.

It turned out the girls were in their early twenty’s and worked at Coyote Ugly. Stacy’s mother bought the boat for her and her friend Barbie. I didn't know it at the time, but over the years we would become good friends.

We finished our rolls and talked a while longer. Diane was a very intelligent girl. She made a good shrink and enjoyed practicing on me every chance she had.

"Let's do this every Sunday," I said.

"Okay," she agreed.

I thought we wouldn't, but we did.

"I have to go now," she said. "I have a date."

"A date?" I asked.

"Yes, you do know I date, don't you?"

"Well, yes but its Sunday."

"What's that got to do with it?"

"Where would you go on a Sunday?"

"Everything's open, just like any other day, Cam."

"Who's the lucky guy?"

"Jack."

I sat up and looked at her.

"Not that Jack," she said and laughed.

"You did that on purpose," I said.

"I know," she said, stood and kissed me on the cheek.

She reached out her hand and said, “Come on.”

I took her hand and stood. “Where we going?”

“I’m going to introduce you to your new neighbors.”

“I’ll meet ‘em in due time,” I said.

“Now,” she said. “If I leave it to you, you’ll say something stupid. You have to live here, you know.”

We walked to the girl's boat holding hands. Secretly, I was glad Diane was there to guide me. I didn’t want the girls to get the impression I was a dirty old man, and I knew I *could* possibly say something stupid.

“Hello,” Diane said. “Welcome to the neighborhood. Do you need any help?”

“No thanks, we’re good,” one of them said. She stuck out her hand and said: “I’m Stacy.”

The other girl said, “Hi, I’m Barbie.”

Diane shook their hands and said, “I’m Diane, and this is my father, Cam.”

I turned red. She could have said, “My friend,” or “My brother,” or something like that. They shook my hand and said, “Nice to meet you, sir.”

The girls were clad in small bikinis, and I had to try not to look. Now I really felt like a dirty old man.

"You sure don't look old enough to be her father," Stacy said.

"Actually, I'm not," I said. "I'm her sugar daddy."

Now Diane turned red. The two girls stared at me wide-eyed.

"I told you, you would say something stupid, Cam," Diane said.

I laughed. "Sorry girls," I said. "Just kidding. I like to embarrass her when I can."

They laughed. "Would you like to join us for a drink?" Barbie said.

"Cam can join you," Diane said. "I have a date. It was nice meeting you. I'm here a lot so I'll see you around."

"Okay," they both said. "Next time stay for a drink."

Diane looked at me and shook her head, "Try not to say anything else," she said.

"I won't," I said.

When Diane left I stepped onto the boat with the girls.

"Where are you girls from?" I asked.

"Texas," Stacy said. "Houston."

"Where are you from, Cam?" Barbie asked.

"Key West," I said. "Born and raised."

"Oh good, maybe you would show us around. We work at Coyote Ugly, but we haven't started yet. We just got here."

"I'd be honored girls."

"You're hot for an older guy," Stacy said.

"Thank you, I think."

"I didn't mean you were old," she said, now a little embarrassed.

"That's okay," I said. "Compared to you, I am."

"Maybe we could go out sometime," Stacy said.

"I'm married," I said. "But thank you."

Chapter 13

Sheriff Buck and I had worked together a few times on some of my cases. We worked well together, and he was quite helpful in my search for Malinda. If I had a lead, I could turn it over to him and he would check it out. None of the leads ever amounted to anything, so he saved me a lot of time.

Though I wanted to spend all my time trying to find the men responsible for Malinda's disappearance, I couldn't. I had bills to pay.

I received a call from Tiff Riley. She's a local realtor here in Key West. Although I've never met her, I feel as if I know her.

I've been looking at her picture on bus stop benches and TV commercials for the last ten years. She's quite attractive and has a radiant smile.

She said her husband hasn't been home for four days. He went out fishing for the day, supposedly with a friend, and he hadn't returned. His friend, however, was at home and confessed he didn't have any plans to go fishing that day.

Tiff came to my houseboat on Wednesday morning to meet with me. She didn't want a PI showing up at her office. She explained that this was on the 'down low.' She didn't want any negative publicity.

I was sitting on the lanai having my third cup of coffee when I heard the warning squeak of the dock gate.

A moment later Tiff appeared at my gangway. At least I think it was Tiff. She didn't look anything like the picture I've been staring at for ten years. Tiff was now a heavier, by at least fifty pounds, version of the vibrant young girl on the billboards. She wore too much jewelry, and her perfume arrived fifteen feet ahead of her. She had a colorful scarf wrapped around her neck. It looked out of place in all this heat. I guessed her age at around forty-eight.

I stood to greet her.

We shook hands and took a seat at the table.

"Would you like something to drink?" I offered.

"I would," she said. "But it's a little early."

I chuckled.

"How can I help you?" I asked.

"My husband," she said, "Like I told you on the phone, he's a gonner, splitsville, runoff with that hussy probably."

"Hussy?"

"Flo," she said. "Can you believe it, Flo. She sounds like the type who take your husband on a one-way spin."

"A one-way spin?"

"Yeah, twirl him around and let 'em go. That offer still on for a drink?"

"What would you like?" I asked.

"What you got?"

"Wild Turkey."

"Straight up," she said.

I fixed us both a drink. It was a little early, but I didn't want her to drink alone.

“Here you are,” I said handing her drink to her and turning to get mine off the bar.

When I turned back, she was holding out an empty glass.

“One more?”

“Sure,” I said and poured another double shot into her glass.

This one she sipped as we talked.

Tiff didn’t come from money, but her husband did, and he has a lot of it. She was a young beauty who won his affection by taking her clothes off in his car on their first date. He was still driving when she, “Took the notion to get naked.”

He nearly wrecked his Cadillac pulling into a parking lot. It was broad daylight and the top was down. They made mad passionate love to a small crowd of spectators.

Why she told me all this, I don’t know, but it was amusing. I’ll never look at another one of her bus stop benches again in the same way.

When she finished her story I said, “Does Flo have a last name?”

“Flo who?” she said.

"Flo who skedaddled with your husband," I said jokingly.

"There ain't no Flo. That was just a metaphor," she said. "It means, *whore.*"

"I see," I said, but I was getting a little confused.

"I don't know if he really has a girlfriend or not. But I don't know any other reason he would leave *me*," she said sitting up straighter and posing. I think.

"Were the two of you fighting before he left?"

"Nope."

"What were you doing?"

"I was beating his truck with a hammer," she said matter-of-factually.

"Why?"

"Cause he was going fishing and it was our twenty-fifth anniversary."

"But you weren't fighting?"

"Nope. He told me he was going fishing. I went out to the driveway and started beating his truck. He came out and got in the truck and said: "See ya." Then he left."

"Did he take his fishing pole?"

"No. I forgot to tell ya. I broke it in half."

"And you don't know any reason he would want to leave you?" I said. The sarcasm going right over her head.

"No, we were happily married for fifteen years."

"But you said you were married for twenty-five years," I said.

"We were."

I downed the rest of my drink. She did the same.

"It's a dry day, ain't it," she said holding her glass out again.

I refilled it. None for me.

"Where do think he might have gone?" I asked.

"Probably to Miami," she said.

"Why there?"

"We have another house there."

"Did you check?"

"Nope."

I waited for her to elaborate on that. She didn't.

"Why not check there first. Then if you can't find him, hire a PI."

"I don't want to be the one to find him. I want him to know I was so worried I had to *hire* someone to find him."

"Do you have any children he might be visiting?"

"We have a fourteen-year-old daughter, but she lives at home," she said.

I could see something change in her eyes at the mention of her daughter.

In surrender, I opened my notebook and asked her for the address. I've had some crazy requests over the years, and this one ranks right up there at the top of the list.

I wrote down the address and told her I would check on him this afternoon.

"Thank you," she said but didn't get up.

"Anything else?" I said

She smiled at me. "Do you have a girlfriend or a wife?" she said sticking her breasts out a little further.

"A girlfriend," I lied.

"Wanna fool around anyway?" and batted her eyes.

"No, but thank you. I'm a one girl kind of guy."

"Too bad," she said. "If I took my clothes off, would you change your mind?"

"As tempting as that is, no," I said.

"Bummer," she said and stood.

We shook hands again. I didn't think she was going to let go. I pulled away gently. She smiled.

Chapter 14

I miss my airplane. I always enjoyed flying it to Miami. Now I have to make the three hours drive through the keys in 92-degree heat. I put the top down anyway.

The drive went smoothly today. Sometimes it can be terrible. You can easily sit in the heat for half an hour, especially if there's a wreck.

I had the address in my Garmin and it directed me to a ritzy neighborhood close to the ocean.

The house was located behind an eight-foot iron fence with a sliding gate, mounted on wheels, and powered by an electric motor.

There was a catwalk around the second story, from which I was sure, would give you a panoramic view of the ocean.

I pressed the buzzer on the intercom and waited for a response. There was none. I tried again. Nothing again.

I punched in the code Tiff had given me and watched the iron gate roll to the right. I entered, parking behind a red Ford truck with about a hundred little dents in the body and hood.

She had done a number on it with that hammer.

Walking to the door, I observed the silence. There was no traffic noise inside the gates. The tall privacy hedges did their job at absorbing sound.

I was going to ring the doorbell but there was none. I surmised with a gate, which had to be opened for you, there was no need for further announcement of your arrival.

I knocked anyway. Still no answer. I tried the door. It swung open.

"*Hello*," I said sticking my head in through the open doorway.

Nothing but silence. Actually, the silence was deafening, if that's possible.

I stepped into the foyer and said, "*Hello*," again.

My voice echoed through the large mansion. The only sound was my own voice dying out as it bounced off the walls and marble floor.

The hair stood up on the back of my neck and arms. I didn't like this feeling. I felt I was invading someone's life, unannounced.

I thought about how I would feel if I came walking around the corner from another room and someone was standing in my house.

"*Hello*," I said a little louder this time, "*Anyone here?*"

Only echoes again.

I decided to search the house. I was a little concerned that the alarm didn't go off when I had entered. Tiff had given me the code for it as well.

The rooms had the resemblance of a majestic hotel lobby, high ceilings, and marble walls. A large oil painting of Tiff was displayed in, what I guessed, was the gathering room.

There was that noise again. As Simon and Garfunkel would say, "The Sound of Silence."

I pushed open a door, which was mounted on self-closing hinges and stepped into the kitchen. The door slowly closed behind me.

The kitchen fit the house. I could live in it, that is if it weren't for the body lying on the floor in a puddle of dried blood.

Jerry Riley the Third, lay on the cold tile floor on his back. His head was smashed in on one side and his brain had partially slid out of the open cavity. Blood covered a good six-foot area around his upper body.

My first thought was, *Is this why Tiff didn't want to be the one to find him?*

I looked around the room from where I stood. There was no sign of a struggle. Whoever did this was an acquaintance of Jerry's.

I backed out of the room letting the door close itself on the macabre setting on the other side.

I used the house phone to call 911, and then wiped off anything I might have touched, and exited the house and grounds before the police arrived.

I knew there could be a chance that I would be the main star in a surveillance video, but I also knew that if Tiff had anything to do with this, the camera would be off. She wouldn't want it to catch her leaving after murdering her husband.

I drove back to Key West. It was eight-fifteen by the time I returned. It was starting to get dark.

Chapter 15

I called Diane first and told her the whole story in case I was arrested. That way I wouldn't have to tell her at the police station while others were listening.

"Do you want an alibi?" she asked.

"No, I don't think it will come to that."

"What will you do?"

"I think I'll call Tiff and see if she's heard from Jerry yet."

"That was three hours ago," Diane said. "Surely the police have visited her by now."

"Yes, you would think so. I guess we'll see."

"I want you to call Jack. You're going to need a witness to every move you make now."

I knew she was right, but I didn't want to drag Jack into this. Something wasn't quite right. I felt as though I was being set up.

I called Tiff.

"Cam," she said. "What did you find out?"

"I haven't gone yet," I said. "I wanted to let you know I'll go first thing in the morning. I got a little tied up."

"But you have to go tonight," she said.

"What difference will one night make?" I said.

There was silence on the line. I waited.

"Would you like to go with me in the morning?" I said. "You can wait in the car and I'll come to get you after I've talked to him."

"No. I told you I don't want to go," she said emphatically.

"Alright," I said. "I'll call you when I get there."

"Mister Derringer, please go tonight. I can't bear one more night without knowing what happened to him."

"Do you think something happened to him?" I asked.

Silence again.

"He's a dreadful man," she finally said.

"Dreadful? How so?"

Silence.

"May I come to your house and talk with you again?"

"Do you think that's necessary?" she asked.

"Yeah, I do."

Silence.

"I'll be there in thirty minutes," I said and hung up.

I called Jack. Diane was right. If she's trying to set me up, I'll need a witness.

"Jack," I said. "Can you spare an hour?"

"Not a problem," he said. "What's up?"

I filled him in.

"I'll run a quick check on him and meet you there in half an hour," he said.

I arrived at her home on Noah Lane. It was a beautiful conch style house and right on the beach.

Jack pulled up the same time I did. I met him at his car.

"Did you find anything interesting?" I asked.

"Maybe," he said. "Did you know they were separated and she's filed for divorce?"

"No, she didn't mention that. Maybe that's why the police haven't contacted her yet."

I knocked on her door. It was answered by their fourteen-year-old daughter. She didn't say anything. She just stared. Her eyes looked frightened and defeated.

"Is your mother home?" I asked.

She nodded her head and stepped aside, allowing us to enter. After closing the door, she led us into the living room and out a set of sliding doors to the pool area.

Tiff was sitting on a chaise lounge with a drink in her hand, and still wearing the scarf, staring at the pool.

"Have a seat, please," she said motioning toward the pool chairs nearby.

"Thank you," I said, and I introduced Jack to her.

"Afraid to come alone?" she said smiling.

"Should I be?"

"Kim, would you get these gentlemen something to drink."

"No, thank you," I said.

"What about you Jack," she said. "You look like a partier."

"Thanks," he said, "I'm good."

She laughed softly. Not like a funny laugh, but more like a, I'm fed up with life laugh.

So, what do you want to talk about?"

"Maybe we should talk somewhere a little more private," Jack said.

"Kim's heard it all before," she said.

I looked at Kim. She just sat on her chair and wrapped her hair around her finger and released it again.

"First," I said. "Why were you trying to find your husband after you kicked him out of the house and filed for divorce?"

Tiff and Kim exchanged a fleeting glance.

"He owes me money," she said.

"Why didn't you just tell me that? I look for deadbeat husbands all the time."

"I was a little embarrassed, and I'm trying to keep it out of the media."

"I'm discrete."

"I hope so. You know, if you did enter my house in Miami, the cameras would have been off."

"Yes, it's a very nice house. I wasn't crazy about the kitchen, but our tastes might differ," I said.

"Like I said, he was a dreadful man."

"Did you send me there hoping I would get blamed for the murder?"

"I don't really know. My plan was a little blurry," she said.

"And it wasn't murder," Kim said.

We all looked at her.

"Were you there?" I asked.

She pulled her long blonde hair away from her face revealing a cut and bruise on her cheek.

"I was there," she said. "I was right under him. He raped me and then beat me. This was the first time he hit me, but he's been coming to my bedroom for two years."

She said all of this somewhat nonchalantly. Like she was talking about it happening to someone else.

Tiff was crying now, "I didn't know," she said. "Kim never told me."

"Was he your biological father?" I asked Kim.

"No, he's my stepdad, but he's the only father I've ever known."

"Jerry didn't know I was in the house," Tiff said. "I came to pick Kim up. She had spent the weekend with him. I heard Kim crying and Jerry yelling at her. When I went into the bedroom he was pulling his pants up and Kim was naked on the bed, her face bleeding."

I looked at Kim. She still had no expression on her face.

Tiff went on, "Jerry looked at me and smirked, "At least one of you will still fuck me," and he laughed.

Chapter 16

We sat in silence for a minute. My mind wandered back to Susie and the way her father pimped her out.

I didn't feel any remorse when I killed him, and I'm sure Tiff doesn't now. Dallas was the same. He needed to rape and kill young girls. He's dead now also. One at a time, we rid the world of these men and life goes on.

"What happened in the kitchen?" I heard Jack ask, bringing me out of my trance.

Tiff and Kim looked at each other again. Kim nodded.

"If you're working for me, can you turn me into the police?"

"I'm not a lawyer anymore so, yes I could."

"Will you?"

"Tell me your story."

"Let's go inside," she said.

We went into the living room and Kim turned on the TV.

"When I saw what Jerry had done," Tiff said, "I turned on the house camera. I was afraid he might not stop there. When we left, I brought the tape with me and turned the camera off."

Kim pushed a button on the remote and the screen lit up revealing a picture with ten different rooms, each with a view of the whole room.

It showed Tiff with her arms around a naked Kim walking to the Master Bedroom and closing the door. Kim put on some of her mother's clothes and they sat on the bed and talked.

Then Tiff got up and stormed out of the bedroom. On another screen, I could see Jerry in the kitchen making himself a drink. Tiff disappeared from one picture and then appeared in the kitchen with Jerry.

They argued, and Tiff slapped him. He hit her in the stomach and then put his hands around her neck.

I glanced at her, *the scarf*.

He bent her backward over the kitchen island and was choking her. I couldn't tell what he was saying but he was yelling.

"He said he was going to kill me," Tiff said as if reading my thoughts. "I was starting to black out."

I could see her going limp. She didn't have but a few more seconds to live.

I was concentrating so hard on the brutal attack that I didn't notice Kim until I saw the blood spray and Jerry hit the floor.

Kim was standing behind him with a fireplace poker raised and ready for another strike. It wouldn't be necessary.

Kim turned off the TV.

No one spoke.

Finally, after a full two minutes, Tiff said, "What now?"

"That depends on the two of you," I said. "Do you want to go through the rest of your life looking over your shoulder for the police to come, or do you want to go settle this right now?"

"What's going to happen to us?" Kim said.

She was very mature for fourteen. I guess she had to grow up quick.

"Luckily for you, you turned on the recorder. I'll go to the police with you, we'll show them the tape and I think you'll walk back out with me."

"This was clearly a case of a girl saving her mother from being murdered," I said.

"I couldn't agree more," Jack said. "There's not a prosecutor in the world that would go after you for this."

"I might not be a lawyer any longer," I said, "but I know the law and I still have clout in the legal system."

It turned out I was right. They did leave with me two hours later. I gave Diane's card to Tiff and strongly advised them to make an appointment with her, together.

Diane told me two weeks later that it was a good thing they came for help. Tiff felt guilty for not seeing what was happening to

Kim. Kim felt guilty for everything, though none of it was her fault.

They'll be okay, but it will take a while. And yes, life goes on.

Chapter 17

One month later, I was sitting on my lanai having my morning coffee. It was Sunday.

I heard the warning squeak from the dock gate and I smiled. Although I've never asked her to, Diane shows up with our chocolate honey buns from Betty's Bakery every Sunday morning.

"Hey ya, Cam," she said and kissed me.

"Hey ya, yourself," I said. "This is a surprise."

"Yeah, right. As if you didn't expect me."

She dropped the Sunday newspaper on the table and sat a white sack down next to it.

I got our milk and napkins. We sat on the fantail and solved the world problems again, just as we do every Sunday. This was by far my favorite time of the week.

"What's new on the case?" she asked as she always does, referring to the boat jacking and Malinda.

"I have a lead on a boat down at the Galleon Marina. I think I'm getting close to finding who is behind all this."

"That would be great," Diane said. "It's time for closure. Not to mention time for those bastards to pay for what they did."

We sat quietly and watched the fish jump and boats slowly come and go.

"Have you talked to Stacy and Barbie lately?" Diane asked.

"They're coming over tonight for drinks and appetizers."

"Are you going to behave?"

"I'll be the perfect gentleman. Would you like to join us?"

"I might if something better doesn't come along."

"I feel so privileged."

"You want another roll?"

"You mean we have more?"

"Yep, I thought it felt like one of those kinds of days."

"Don't mind if I do."

We sat quietly and ate our second roll, then Diane said, "I love you, Cam."

I felt a lump in my throat. I knew she still missed her parents and sometimes it was overwhelming for her. She knew I was still grieving for Malinda too. After everything else, the pain, the heartbreak all the difficulties, we still had each other. I prayed we always would.

"I love you too, Diane."

We sat in silence again and finished our rolls.

"That felt sinful, eating two, didn't it?" Diane said.

"Yeah, I guess I'll run an extra mile today."

"I'm running with Jack today," she said. "I'll get him to add a mile too."

"When am I going to meet this Jack?"

"I'm talking about your Jack, Cam."

"What! No, no, no."

"It's not a date. We'll only be out on the streets running."

"Call me when you get back," I said sternly.

Diane laughed, stood and kissed me.

"I'll be here for drinks tonight," she said.

I hugged her. "Be careful out there running," I said.

"Bye," she said as she walked down the dock.

"*Thanks for the rolls*," I called after her.

She waved.

"*Call me*!" I yelled.

When Diane was gone I opened the newspaper and read the local news. There was always something happening in Key West. No murders reported today. The town has become tamer as the years go by, unlike other towns that have become more dangerous.

I turned to the obituaries. I'm always nervous when I read them since I have a lot of old friends here and I've seen a few of their faces in this section over the years.

This time there was only one who I recognized, my old teacher, Mr. Powers. He died in bed surrounded by his three daughters and wife. He was sixty-five. I did some math in my head and realized that he was only twenty-five when I saw him outside Susie's window. At the time, I thought of him as an old man. I guess compared to a twelve-year-old boy, he was.

I had no feelings one way or the other now. I was sorry for his children for losing their father, but at the same time I couldn't help but wonder if he had abused them. I had no way to know, so I didn't judge him on that.

Life goes on.

Chapter 18

I had a lunch date with a potential client at noon. I wore my best suit and actually put on dress shoes. I felt awkward in so many clothes, but we were meeting at Latitudes on Sunset Key and I had to dress for it. Not to mention the client was the beautiful Irene Silver.

Her father owned marinas from Key West to Key Largo. I wasn't sure how many, but I knew the family was worth well over five-hundred-million.

They were having problems with some of their boats being stolen and knew I was working on a related case. Irene thought we might be able to help one another.

We had met a few times through Malinda. They would have luncheons occasionally and worked on a few charities together.

I arrived first, and the waiter led me to what is considered the VIP table. It had a beautiful view of The Gulf of Mexico and the palm tree strewn beach. Irene had chosen the table. She only lived a few houses away.

For her, it was a short walk, or golf cart ride, for me an eight-minute boat ride. Not bad for a great escape.

I watched her walk across the room, as all the men did, toward me. I stood, and we hugged.

She was dressed in a magenta Cushnie Et Ochs Cutout-Neck Fitted Stretch-Cady Cocktail Dress with Flutter Detail.

No, I'm not a clothes snob. Malinda had one similar to it in white and would tell me what it was every time she put it on. She would always say in a sexy voice, "Fifteen hundred dollars." It was her favorite.

"Cam, so good to see you again. I can't believe we don't get together once in a while."

"Life always gets in the way," I said.

"That it does. How are things?" she said, her expression changing as it does for anyone when they inquire.

I know they want to ask how I'm doing without Malinda but don't want to come right out and ask.

"Things are good, Irene. Diane is keeping me busy."

"She's such a lovely girl," she said. The fact that she's older than Diane by four years showed in her voice.

We ordered a bottle of wine and then our entrees while we made small talk.

It was hard to concentrate with her sitting across the table. Not only was she a classic beauty, but the dress.

"As hard as it is to talk business here," I said, "I think we should."

"You're not going to be a party pooper, are you?" she said with a crooked smile.

"Business first," I said.

"Okay. Well, we've had twelve boats stolen in the last four months. It's not unusual to have a couple heisted, but this is getting out of hand. Sometimes they show up just drifting in the bay or the gulf and other times we never see them again."

"Have you had anyone investigate yet?"

"The coast guard, the sheriff's department and the local police. It's time for action though so I called the best." She smiled again while I felt her foot rub my leg.

I pulled back–slightly.

"Has anyone been hurt in any of the jacking's?" I asked.

"Probably," she said. "The last boat we found had quite a bit of blood on it."

"Where was the boat from?"

"Islamorada."

"Can you get me a list of the registration numbers of the boats that are missing?"

She opened her purse and pulled out a folded paper with the list on it.

"Are we finished with our meeting now?" she said and rubbed my leg again.

I agreed to walk her home before catching my ferry. At her door, she put her arms around me and kissed me softly.

"Will you come in for a drink?" she said.

I thought about it. The kiss was the first since I kissed Malinda goodbye. It felt good and made things stir, but I felt as if I were cheating on her.

"I'm sorry Irene, I'm just not ready."

"That's okay, Cam. You will be someday, and I'll be here."

She kissed me again, said, "Good luck with the investigation," and disappeared inside the house.

I stood on her front porch for a full minute before turning and leaving.

Irene, leaning against the door inside the house, let out a defeated breath when she heard Cam leave.

I looked over the list of boats while on the ferry and decided to walk the docks once before returning to my boat. I looked a little out of place in my suit and it was hot.

I walked from one dock to the next looking at numbers and names. I knew I wasn't being thorough, but I would come back. I just wanted to see if anything jumped out at me.

It did. There was a forty-two-foot Sea Ray sitting in one of the slips. I could see the name was *"Count Me Inn"* which matched one on the sheet.

I walked around the boat to see the numbers. As I bent down to read them, I heard someone behind me. Before I could turn to see who it was, the lights went out.

I woke somewhere in the dark. I was naked and laying in the mud on a rutted-out gravel road.

A very lovely passerby stopped to help me. She called Diane for me and together they took me to the hospital where I was treated.

The girl's name was Jenny. She stayed around Key West and me for a long while and became a very important piece of the puzzle.

I'm not sure if I'll find the men responsible for Malinda's disappearance, but I do know, I'll never give up.

Too many people have suffered from abuse, and I will keep my solemn promise to not allow it if I can prevent it.

I still grieve for Malinda and Susie, but for Annie, Kimberly, Diane and me, life goes on.

Continued:

This is where the first book in the Cam Derringer series starts. Join Cam in Key West while he manages to get in and out of trouble using his skills both above and below the law. It's a fast action series full of twists and turns with a new challenge around every corner. Beautiful and powerful women, Wild Turkey and a thirst for action make Cam Derringer a man you'll want to follow.

Written by Mac Fortner, the Best-Selling Author of the Cam Derringer and Sunny Ray Series.

You can read the series by following this link:

https://amzn.to/2LSdv1F

CAM DERRINGER SERIES:

KNEE DEEP–Book 1
BLOODSHOT–Book 2
KEY WEST: TWO BIRDS ONE STONE: Book 3
Coming soon:
MURDER FEST KEY WEST–Book 4

KNEE DEEP is also available on AUDIO

SUNNY RAY SERIES:

RUM CITY BAR–Book 1
BATTLE FOR RUMORA–Book 2

Made in the USA
Middletown, DE
01 December 2019